anythink

D0384880

Holly and Hank's Snow Holiday

The Sound of H

by Joanne Meier and Cecilia Minden • illustrated by Bob Ostrom

The Child's World

Published by The Child's World®
1980 Lookout Drive
Mankato, MN 56003-1705
800-599-READ
www.childsworld.com

The Child's World®: Mary Berendes, Publishing Director
The Design Lab: Design and page production

Library of Congress Cataloging-in-Publication Data
Meier, Joanne D.
  Holly and Hank's snow holiday : the sound of h /
by Joanne Meier and Cecilia Minden ; illustrated by
Bob Ostrom.
    p. cm.
  ISBN 978-1-60253-403-2 (library bound : alk. paper)
  1. English language—Consonants—Juvenile literature.
2. English language—Phonetics— literature 3. Reading—
Phonetic method—Juvenile literature. I. Minden, Cecilia.
II. Ostrom, Bob. III. Title.
  PE1159.M457 2010
  [E]—dc22   2010002916

Printed in the United States of America in Mankato, MN.
July 2010
F11538

NOTE TO PARENTS AND EDUCATORS:

The Child's World® has created this series with the goal of exposing children to engaging stories and illustrations that assist in phonics development. The books in the series will help children learn the relationships between the letters of written language and the individual sounds of spoken language. This contact helps children learn to use these relationships to read and write words.

The books in this series follow a similar format. An introductory page, to be read by an adult, introduces the child to the phonics feature, or sound, that will be highlighted in the book. Read this page to the child, stressing the phonic feature. Help the student learn how to form the sound with her mouth. The story and engaging illustrations follow the introduction. At the end of the story, word lists categorize the feature words into their phonic elements.

Each book in this series has been carefully written to meet specific readability requirements. Close attention has been paid to elements such as word count, sentence length, and vocabulary. Readability formulas measure the ease with which the text can be read and understood. Each book in this series has been analyzed using the Spache readability formula.

Reading research suggests that systematic phonics instruction can greatly improve students' word recognition, spelling, and comprehension skills. This series assists in the teaching of phonics by providing students with important opportunities to apply their knowledge of phonics as they read words, sentences, and text.

This is the letter h.

In this book, you will read words that have the **h** sound as in: *home, helping, hands,* and *hat.*

Holly and Hank are home from school.

They are making a snowman!

Holly is helping Hank.

"Here, use your hands like this," says Holly. "This is how you roll the snow."

Hank rolls three heavy snowballs. He carries them to Holly.

"Now he needs a hat on his head," says Holly. Hank puts a hat on the snowman's head.

"Let's give him a happy face," says Holly.

"Here!" says Hank.

"Here are some buttons."

Hank helps Holly make

a button face.

The snowman is done.

"Let's take him home!"

says Hank.

"The snowman has to stay here," says Holly. "He is too heavy to move. Bye-bye!"

Fun Facts

You wave your hand when you want to say hello or good-bye, and you might clap your hands when you applaud for a performer on stage. But some people use their hands to communicate all of the time. People who are deaf learn to spell with their hands or move their hands in a certain way to express themselves.

People have been wearing hats for a very long time! The remains of Egyptian mummies reveal that ancient people frequently wore hats and headdresses. People wear hats today to shade their eyes from the sun or to keep their heads warm. Thousands of years ago hats symbolized much more. At that time, the type of hat a person wore showed whether that individual was rich or poor, powerful or not important.

Activity

Learning How to Talk with Your Hands
Even if you don't know someone who is deaf, you still might enjoy learning sign language. Your local library should have several books with illustrations that show the different hand signs and what they mean. Ask a friend to learn the signs with you. That way, you can practice speaking with one another.

To Learn More

Books
About the Sound of H
Moncure, Jane Belk. *My "h" Sound Box®*. Mankato, MN: The Child's World, 2009.

About Hands
Haan, Amanda, and Marina Sagona (illustrator). *I Call My Hand Gentle*. New York: Viking, 2003.
Ross, Tony. *Wash Your Hands*. Brooklyn: Kane/Miller, 2000.

About Hats
Keats, Ezra Jack. *Jennie's Hat*. New York: Viking, 2003.
Morris, Ann, and Ken Heyman (photographer). *Hats, Hats, Hats*. New York: Mulberry Books, 1993.

About Helping
Brown, Marc Tolon. *Arthur Helps Out*. New York: Little, Brown, 2005.
Snow, Todd, and Melodee Strong (illustrator). *You Are Helpful*. Oak Park Heights, MN: Maren Green, 2008.

Web Sites
Visit our home page for lots of links about the Sound of H:
childsworld.com/links

Note to Parents, Teachers, and Librarians: We routinely check our Web links to make sure they're safe, active sites—so encourage your readers to check them out!

H Feature Words

Proper Names

Hank

Holly

Feature Words in Initial Position

hand

happy

has

hat

he

head

heavy

help

helping

here

him

his

home

how

About the Authors

Joanne Meier, PhD, has worked as an elementary school teacher, university professor, and researcher. She earned her BA in early childhood education from the University of South Carolina, and her MEd and PhD in education from the University of Virginia. She currently works as a literacy consultant for schools and private organizations. Joanne lives in Virginia with her husband Eric, daughters Kella and Erin, two cats, and a gerbil.

Cecilia Minden, PhD, is the former director of the Language and Literacy Program at the Harvard Graduate School of Education. She is now a reading consultant for school and library publications. She earned her PhD in reading education from the University of Virginia. Cecilia and her husband, Dave Cupp, live outside Chapel Hill, North Carolina. They enjoy sharing their love of reading with their grandchildren, Chelsea and Qadir.

About the Illustrator

Bob Ostrom has been illustrating children's books for nearly twenty years. A graduate of the New England School of Art & Design at Suffolk University, Bob has worked for such companies as Disney, Nickelodeon, and Cartoon Network. He lives in North Carolina with his wife Melissa and three children, Will, Charlie, and Mae.